Paul Diggens
Illustrations by Ted Toms

Tom Tunnel

Bumblebee Books
London

A CIP catalogue record for this title is
available from the British Library.

ISBN: 978-1-83934-610-1

Bumblebee Books is an imprint of
Olympia Publishers.

First Published in 2022

Bumblebee Books
Tallis House
2 Tallis Street
London
EC4Y 0AB

Printed in Great Britain

www.olympiapublishers.com

Dedication

Dedicated to Lewis, Rio, Rhys, Tia and Mason, grandchildren who love the *Tom Tunnel* stories.

Tom Tunnel is a curious old railway tunnel hardly ever used today. He resides in a hilly part in the middle of England. Around him are the rolling hills of the lovely countryside.

'I was made many years ago,' said Tom Tunnel. 'Yes, I am well over one hundred years young. I am very worn but still very strong. All my bricks were brought here by horse and cart. They were special bricks too as they have kept me together all these years.'

'When I was young, they laid railway track in my belly. Some trains with lots of smoke passed through me making me cough a bit. I am not really a smoking tunnel. They found a lot of smoke in me when steam trains went through so they dug a big chimney. It goes up into the hill to let the smoke out,' said Tom.

'I used to enjoy life when the trains went through. Even in the near darkness I could see people's faces at the windows. The carriages were bright and at summertime passengers seemed to be very happy. They might have been on their holidays.'

'Let me show you around. My important entrance is to the south. Here I can see the lovely landscape of fields going for miles and miles. In the distance the church spire of a far-flung town.

So I'll turn my head and show you the other entrance is to the north. It's a bit colder this way round. When the cold winds blow it can make me chilly. In the winter-time the snowmen come and visit me.'

But Tom Tunnel had suffered during his life-time. It was a normal day but the clouds were dark. The wind was cool. The sky got darker and darker, the birds stopped singing and then it happened.

'My belly moved, first just a little,' said Tom Tunnel, 'then lots and lots – all the earth moved. I was shaken around so, so much. It seemed endless but it only lasted a few seconds. The earth moved so much. I really didn't know what happened. some of my roof bricks came unstuck and fell out.'

Then the birds began to sing, the clouds cleared to a sunny day. Tom Tunnel was puzzled as to what had just happened. Inside his south facing tunnel entrance lived Bertie the bat in a nest high up in one of the earthy gaps in the roof.

'What's just happened, Bertie?' asked Tom Tunnel. 'It was very scary and it moved my belly about – I feel a bit sicky.' Bertie Bat was worried!

'Do not fear,' said Bertie the Bat, 'we've just had a minor earthquake. It's all good now.'

'That's a relief, 'said Tom Tunnel, 'but some of my roof bricks have fallen down. I need a repair man, it's a worry.' Within an hour two men walk into the tunnel with a very bright light. After a few minutes they saw the problem. Three giant bricks had fallen from the roof onto the railway tracks.

'Right,' said the inspector, 'we will stop any trains and get the tunnel repaired.'

Tom Tunnel felt a bit weak and sore. 'My roof is damaged and I'm a bit sore,' he said.

'Don't worry,' said Bertie Bat, 'they will sort you out very soon.'

'I'm so sore,' said Tom Tunnel, 'my roof hurts.' The night came and Tom Tunnel tried to get to sleep but his roof hurt lots and lots. Tom Tunnel turned a nasty colour of dark purple and went to sleep.

A day later special bricklayers turned up and started the repairs. They carefully lifted the bricks and put them back in Tom Tunnels roof. The work took a whole day but it was all done by nightfall and the bricklayers went home.

It was almost night-time and Tom Tunnel had been asleep all day. Bertie Bat fluttered around. 'Wake up, Tom Tunnel,' said Bertie Bat, 'the men have fixed your roof.'

With a large yawn Tom Tunnel woke up and straight away said, 'I feel better, my aches are all gone. Thank you, Bertie, for waking me up.'

And with that life returned to normal for Tom Tunnel. An occasional goods train passed through his tunnel and life was good, but what's going to happen to Tom Tunnel at Easter??

About the Author

Paul Diggens has had extensive experience in many of life's roles – as a pirate radio operator, a clerk in the telephone manager's office, a journalist and press officer with the post office and for many years, Head of PR and media. Following his post office career, Paul became involved with the railways with route filming and creating DVDs for enthusiasts. During his time travelling he came up with the idea of children's books centred around Tom Tunnel. He sincerely hopes you enjoy the stories and great illustrations from his long term friend and colleage Ted Toms.

Photo www.225studios.com